The HAVE A GOOD DAY CAFE

by Frances Park and Ginger Park

illustrations by Katherine Potter

LEE & LOW BOOKS Inc.
New York

Manufactured in China

Book design by Mina Greenstein
Book production by The Kids at Our House

The text is set in Cushing
The illustrations are rendered in pastel

(HC) 10 9 8 7 6 5 4 3 2
(PB) 10 9 8 7 6 5 4 3 2 1
First Edition

Library of Congress Cataloging-in-Publication Data
Park, Frances.
      The Have a Good Day Cafe / by Frances Park and Ginger Park ;
illustrations by Katherine Potter.— 1st ed.
          p. cm.
Summary: Mike's grandmother, who has moved from Korea to live
with Mike and his family in the United States, inspires him to suggest
an idea to help their floundering food cart business.
ISBN 978-1-58430-171-4 (hc)   ISBN 978-1-60060-358-7 (pb)
[1. Grandmothers—Fiction. 2. Korean Americans—Fiction. 3. Street
vendors—Fiction.] I. Park, Ginger. II. Potter, Katherine, ill. III. Title.
PZ7.P21976Hav 2005
[E]—dc22   2004011277

To Justin and his grandma—*F.P.* and *G.P.*

For my parents, who set the stage—*K.P.*

Grandma is in the kitchen making a big pot of rice soup. After helping Mom and Dad hitch our food cart to the back of the van, I'm so hungry!

"Mmm," I say. "The *guk bap* smells good."

"Mmm," Grandma says back. "Delicious!"

Last spring Grandma came to America to live with us. We speak mostly in Korean, but Grandma is also learning some English. Her favorite words are *hi, bye,* and *delicious!*

"Daybreak is beautiful here, just like it is back home," Grandma murmurs as she stirs the soup. "Every morning as the sun rose over the rice fields, I would cook delicious food for my whole family." Grandma sighs. "How I miss my country."

"I know, Grandma," I say.

"When you were outside you reminded me of your father when he was seven years old," Grandma tells me. "He would help me carry sacks of rice and vegetables home from the village market."

I feel sorry for Grandma, always daydreaming about the past. The faraway look on her face means she wishes she were back in Korea instead of here with us.

"Help me put breakfast on the table, Mike," Grandma says.

One by one, I carry four steaming bowls of *guk bap* to the table. The wonderful smell of the soup fills the apartment.

"You're the best cook, Grandma," I say.

Grandma winks at me. "You're the best helper, Mike."

After breakfast Dad says to Grandma, "*Omoni,* we must go now."

"Today," Grandma says, "I'm going too."

"*Omoni,*" Dad says, frowning. "It's going to be a hot day. You should stay home and rest your feet in this cool apartment."

"I did not travel ten thousand miles just to stay home and rest my feet day after day. I am tired of resting my feet!" Grandma insists.

We're off to the city.

The streets are bustling with cars and trucks and people going to work. The sun shines brightly over the tall buildings. The clock tower high in the sky chimes seven forty-five.

Mom and Dad set up our food cart at our usual spot on a block that surrounds a park.

"This is a very busy corner," Dad assures Grandma as he sets down her straw mat on a grassy spot under a shade tree. "We have it all to ourselves."

"By lunchtime there will be a parade of people on the sidewalk," Mom adds.

Mom and Dad balance the big umbrella that springs open over the cart before going to work preparing the food. Bagels and orange juice for breakfast. Hot dogs and pizza for lunch. Pretzels and popcorn. These are my favorite American foods.

I take out my crayons and draw a giant slice of pizza. Grandma studies my picture with wide-open eyes.

"Mike, what are those funny red circles?" she asks.

"Pepperoni," I say, giggling. "I love pepperoni!"

"When your father was small, his favorite food was *mandoo*," Grandma says. "I would hold a hot, steaming dumpling up to my lips and make a smile with it. How he would laugh and laugh!"

I laugh too, thinking about a dumpling smile, but I wish Grandma wouldn't daydream about the past so much.

Taxis honk their horns while noisy buses drop off and
pick up passengers. A few people stop for bagels and orange juice.

Soon two other carts set up near our corner.

"Those carts serve the same foods as our cart," Grandma says with
a frown.

"Why are they here?" I ask. "This is *our* corner!"

Mom and Dad exchange worried looks. "I guess the city is allowing other
food carts here now," Dad says.

Grandma fans herself and watches the morning
pass. I'm having fun drawing letters in the colors of
Grandma's fan. I hold up my picture for her to see.

"'I love Grandma,'" I read.

Grandma hugs me. "I love Mike," she says.

By noon a small line forms at our food cart.

One customer orders some chips and a soda.

"Have a good day," Mom says as she hands the man his change.

A second customer orders a hot dog.

"Have a good day," Dad says as he gives the girl her food.

"I like this 'Have a good day' saying," Grandma remarks. "In Korea we say *'Annyonghi kasipsio,'* but it all means the same thing."

Only a few more customers
trickle our way before lunchtime is over.

Heat rises off the sidewalk. Grandma fans
herself so wildly, it seems as if the leaves on the
shade tree are blowing. The rest of the afternoon slowly
ticks by. Every now and then Dad gazes up at the clock tower.
Hours pass—no more customers.

As the sun sets over the sidewalk, Grandma watches me help
Dad hitch up our food cart.

"Slow business today," Grandma comments.

"Too much competition now," Mom says, sounding worried.

Summer days pass like blurry buses whizzing by. Every day Grandma sits on her straw mat and fans herself while I draw pictures.

One cloudy day Mom shakes her head as the two other carts set up. "Not enough business here for three carts," she says. "We need more customers."

"Why don't we move to a new corner?" Grandma asks.

"Because our license says *this* is our corner," Dad explains.

Grandma's forehead wrinkles with concern.

Raindrops begin to fall during lunchtime. Umbrellas open like giant mushrooms. People rush by our food cart and into buildings.

Worry crosses Dad's face as thunder rolls in. "Too many more days like this and we may have to give up our cart," he says.

"And go back to Korea?" Grandma asks with a wishful look.

"Grandma!" I cry. "America is our home now."

The ride home that evening is long and quiet.

Grandma heads for the kitchen to make dinner. "Come help me, Mike," she says.

As I help Grandma make the noodles and sauce for *chajang myun*, I suddenly have an idea. I tell Grandma and she is excited. Together we make a plan.

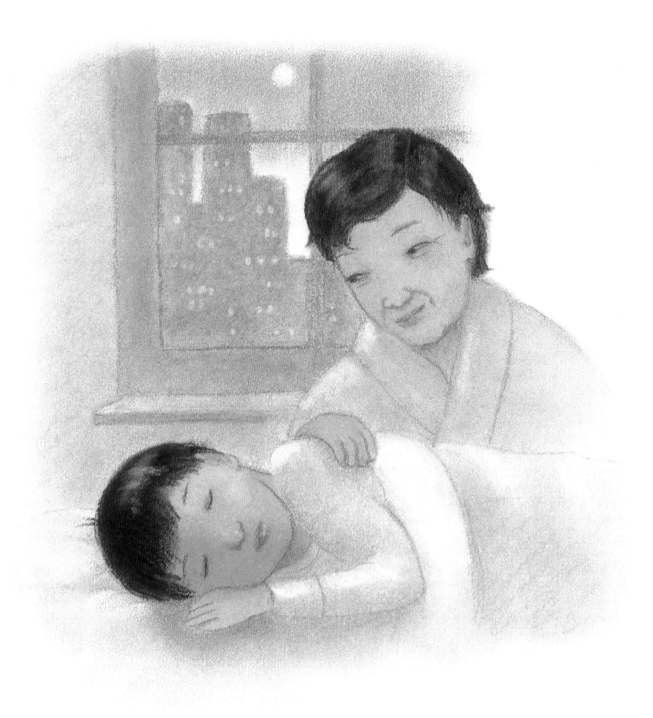

The next morning Grandma wakes me up so early, the moon
is still bright in the sky.

"Today we really *are* going to have a good day," I whisper.

Grandma nods, and we tiptoe down the hall.

In the kitchen Grandma opens the refrigerator. She takes out a big piece of beef, two heads of cabbage, and all the carrots and zucchini she can find. We slice some of the meat for *bulgogi*, then marinate the slices in soy sauce, sesame seeds, and garlic.

We stir-fry cellophane noodles for *chop chae*, then season the dish to perfection.

We roll out dough and stuff *mandoo*.
We chop colorful vegetables for
bibim bap, then whip up the pancake
batter for *jijim*.

The noise wakes up Mom and Dad.

"Why are you two cooking this feast?"
Dad asks sleepily.

"Today we're going to have a new
menu," I say. "Today we'll sell Korean
food from our cart."

Grandma holds a *mandoo* up to her
lips and makes a smile with it. Mom
and Dad smile back and laugh.

In the city, after breakfast, we get ready for
lunchtime. Mom, Dad, and Grandma grill *bulgogi,*
fry *mandoo,* and flip *jijim.* Then they begin putting
out our Korean delicacies.

"Mike, why don't you come help us set
up?" Grandma asks.

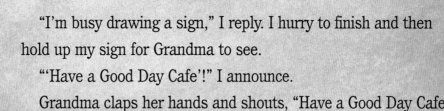

"I'm busy drawing a sign," I reply. I hurry to finish and then hold up my sign for Grandma to see.

"'Have a Good Day Cafe'!" I announce.

Grandma claps her hands and shouts, "Have a Good Day Cafe!"

Mom and Dad chime in. "Have a Good Day Cafe!"

Dad lifts me and I tape my sign to our umbrella for the whole city to see.

Grandma fans herself anxiously as we await the lunch crowd. She fans and fans herself until she is fanning so fast, the aromas of our food travel up and down the street and around the corner.

Soon a chorus of *mmms* comes our way as everyone follows the delicious smells to the Have a Good Day Cafe. A long line forms at our cart.

One customer orders a bowl of *bibim bap*.

"Have a good day," Dad says as he hands her the food.

A second customer orders a platter of *bulgogi* and rice.

"Have a good day," Mom says as she gives the man his change.

A third customer orders *mandoo* and a *jijim*.

"Have a good day!" Grandma and I say together.

The line finally dwindles down at the end of the day. With a purple crayon, Grandma waves me over to her straw mat.

"Mike, let's plan tomorrow's menu," she says.

"How about *naeng myun?*" I suggest. "I love noodles."

Grandma nods. "Sounds good. What about some spicy vegetable side dishes?"

My mouth waters. "Yeah!"

"And *kalbi*," Grandma adds.

"Yum," I say. "I love spareribs too."

Grandma sighs happily. "It's been a good day, Mike."

"A great day," I say, "at the Have a Good Day Cafe!"

Grandma puts her arm around me and hugs me tight. I think she is feeling right at home now.

Learn About the Korean Words in the Story

안녕히 계십시오 Annyonghi kasipsio.
(ahn-nyong-HEE KAH-ship-she-oh) Have a good day.

비빔밥 bibim bap
(BEE-bim bahp) mound of rice topped with seasoned beef, mixed vegetables, and a fried egg

불고기 bulgogi
(PUHL-goh-ghee)
strips of marinated beef

짜장면
chajang myun
(JAH-jahng myong)
noodles smothered in thick brown sauce

잡채
chop chae
(CHOP cheh)
transparent noodles stir-fried with beef and a mixture of colorful vegetables

지짐 jijim *(JEE-jeem)*
pureed bean pancakes with pork and cabbage spiced with red peppers

국밥
guk bap *(KUK bahp)*
rice soup

갈비 **kalbi** *(KAHL-bee)* barbecued beef ribs

만두 **mandoo** *(MAHN-due)* dumplings stuffed with a meat, tofu, and vegetable paste

냉면 **naeng myun** *(NAEHNG myong)* chilled beef broth with noodles, vegetables, slivered pork, and boiled eggs

어머니 **omoni** *(AH-mah-nee)* mother